Troll Hunters is published by Stone Arch Books
A Capstone Imprint
1710 Roe Crest Dr.
North Mankato, Minnesota 56003
www.capstonepub.com

Summary: Dr. Hoo has been kidnapped! The mentor of the young heroes has been taken into the hidden kingdom of the enemy. The teens decide to descend deep underground to rescue him, but they are not prepared for what awaits them in the darkness below…

Designed by Hilary Wacholz

Cataloging-in-Publication Data is available at the Library of Congress website.
ISBN: 978-1-4342-3309-7 (library binding)

Printed in the United States of America in Stevens Point, Wisconsin.
102011
006404WZS12

The Lava Crown

BOOK 3

WRITTEN BY MICHAEL DAHL

ILLUSTRATED BY BEN KOVAR

STONE ARCH BOOKS
www.stonearchbooks.com

TABLE OF CONTENTS

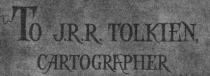

To J.R.R. TOLKIEN,
CARTOGRAPHER

Fiercer than lava,
Stronger than stone,
Harder than iron,
Brighter than bone,
Sharper than teeth,
Deeper than fear —
Answer this, friend,
And see it appear.

— An ancient gathool riddle

BELOW ZION FALLS...

Uzhk resembled something from a nightmare.
The creature's arms and legs moved like
muscular rocks as he clambered down steep,
vertical passageways, traveling deeper
into the earth. With the speed of a lizard,
he scurried along the rock walls, swinging
from one ledge to another. Endless corridors
opened like monstrous throats, revealing
immense caverns and dizzying pits.

Suddenly, he stopped. Stones crumbled
off the trail and fell silently beneath him.
He sniffed the air. His eyes were used to the
ancient darkness, but they couldn't help him
choose his way among the countless paths.
Only his nose guided him through the maze
of prehistoric rock. Again, he sniffed the air.
There was that scent, rising from deep below.

The scent of humans.

1

THE GOLDEN BAND

East of the town of Zion Falls, within a dark wood that lay alongside County Road One, was a large house with a stone tower. And at the top of that tower was a room. And in that room a group of young people were gathered. Their clothes and hair stank from the smoke of a great fire — the lingering traces of a recent battle. They were frightened. The one person they had expected to find in this house, the mysterious Dr. Hoo, had been kidnapped.

Until two days ago, when the stars fell on Zion Falls in a spectacular display of meteors, Zak Fisher would never have let himself be seen with the other kids in the room. Before that night, Zak had never even spoken to Pablo O'Ryan, the nerdy kid from his science class, or Thora Gamble, the track girl. And Mara Lovecraft — he'd never even met her before.

And then there was the little girl who had a flare gun tucked into her dress. Normally, Zak hated little kids, but even eight-year-old Louise was beginning to grow on him. After all they had been through together, Zak was starting to think of them as his friends.

Now, they all sat around Zak. "It doesn't make sense," he said. "Who could've taken Dr. Hoo?"

Mara hesitated. She glanced nervously at Thora. "The *gathool* took him," she said. "He's being held by the trolls now."

The room was silent for a moment. Then Thora leaped to her feet. Her face was red and her fists were clenched. "Say it," she said. "Go ahead, say it! We're all thinking it. The doctor disappeared because my brother took him. That's why his pocket knife is here. Bryce carved *croatoan* into the wall with his knife, then left it here!"

Mara unfolded her arms and stuck her hands in the pockets of her long coat. "I don't know for sure," she said. "But, yes, it looks that way."

Thora covered her face with her hands and stood weeping in the middle of the room. Louise ran over to her and wrapped her small arms around Thora's waist.

Zak's heart sank as he stared at Thora. She had been so brave. She had saved them all from two giant trolls outside the doctor's house the night before. And just a few hours ago, she and Louise had somehow transformed themselves into powerful beings and helped defeat an invasion of even more trolls. Zak himself had been transformed. Pablo, too. They had all become warriors in the fight against the ancient *gathool*, the troll-like creatures from deep within the planet.

But now, Thora looked weak and small. *I guess that's normal*, Zak thought. *After all, the world is basically coming to an end.*

Creatures that Zak had believed only existed in legends and myths were *real*. And they were coming to take back Earth from humans.

"Maybe Bryce was taken too," Pablo said quietly. "Maybe he tried to help Dr. Hoo, but couldn't. Maybe he left his pocket knife here as a sign." Pablo looked back at Thora, who peered at him through the damp strands of her hair. "To let you know where they took him," he added.

Thora sniffed. She wiped the tears from her cheeks. "You think so?" she said.

"Sure," said Pablo. "But I still don't get what that word means." He pointed at the wall. The word *croatoan* was carved deeply into the wood.

Zak crossed his arms. "It doesn't matter what the word means," he said. "What matters is they're both gone, just like my parents. And *we* have to go find them."

Mara shook her head. "It's too dangerous," she said.

"What do you mean?" Zak asked.

"It's likely that the trolls are trying to lure you underground to their realm," Mara said. "It's almost certainly a trap."

"We've defeated the trolls before," argued Zak. "Twice, in fact. The doctor showed us how."

Thora tucked her hair behind her ears. "I agree with Zak," she said. "The doctor saved us. Now we have to save him."

Mara sighed. She looked over at the wooden table near the center of the room. Dr. Hoo's library was crammed with hundreds of books. "I gave those books on the top of the table to Dr. Hoo," she said. Mara walked over, selected one book, and flipped through its pages. She stopped at a particular page and opened the book toward the others.

"Listen to this," Mara said. She read aloud: "An ancient prophecy among the *gathool* has warned them for centuries of a deadly 'band of light' that could destroy their species. But the *gathool* vocabulary is small; their mouths are limited in the sounds they can make. So few words must stand for many things. 'Band' can also mean 'ring' or 'circle.' 'Light' can also stand for 'gold,' 'shining,' or 'pain.'"

Thora nodded. "That's what the doctor read to us the other night," she said. "He said it meant that sunlight could defeat the trolls."

"It turns them to stone," added Pablo.

"It means something else, too," said Mara. "The *gathool* can only be defeated by a 'band of light.' That does refer to the sun, but also means a band of companions."

"Like . . . a rock band?" asked Zak.

Mara shot Zak a confused look. "What? No, of course not," she said.

Zak's face turned red. "Then what *do* you mean?" he asked defensively.

"A band of companions, or friends," Mara said. "A band of warriors. Warriors whose brilliant light can defeat the trolls, just like sunlight.

Just like when Pablo, Louise, Thora and I had radiated light as we battled, Zak thought.

"Dr. Hoo told me that you were chosen for this fight," said Mara. "He's spoken of you all for many years."

"But how?" asked Pablo. "He never met us before last night."

"I'm not sure," Mara said. "But Dr. Hoo was convinced that Zion Falls was going to be the next battleground between the forces of darkness and the forces of light. He knew that the *gathool* would use places in this town as their entry points to the surface."

"Like the old well on the Nye farm," said Pablo.

"And the pit under the silo," said Thora.

Pablo stood up. "We have to get to that old well," he said. "If the trolls have taken Bryce and the doctor underground, then that's how they'd get back to their world."

"What makes you so sure?" asked Zak.

Pablo shook his head. "I don't know," he said. "It just . . . feels right."

Zak stared at Pablo.

Zak glimpsed a weird light in Pablo's eyes. *Starlight.* He had seen it before — and each time, it felt like the two of them were connected.

Zak nodded confidently. "Yeah," he said. "You're right."

"Then it's settled," said Thora. "How far is the well from here?"

Mara stepped forward. "No," she said. Everyone turned to look at her. "You aren't going to the well."

Zak threw up his arms in frustration. "What are you talking about?" he said. "That's the only way underground."

"No," repeated Mara. "It's not. There is a way to the troll's kingdom that is much closer."

Mara took a step toward the wall.

She raised her finger, pointing at the word etched into its surface. "*Croatoan*," she said, "is a *gathool* word that means 'bridge to the underworld'."

Puzzled faces stared back at Mara. She opened her hands to take in all of the tower. "The *gathool* have marked this tower as a gateway to the their kingdom," she explained. "And we're going to use it to enter their world."

2

Drums in the Dark

With each step downward, Bryce Gamble found it harder to breathe. He and the doctor were marching deeper and deeper into the endless tunnels below the earth. The air was thick and hot, and felt heavy like it did before a summer storm in Zion Falls.

Zion Falls? Bryce barely remembered the place anymore. He had a faint memory of the meteor shower that he and his sister Thora had watched at the old quarry outside of town.

How long ago had that been? Days? Years? Only darkness surrounded him now. Darkness and smoke.

Hroooooom . . . hroom . . .

A drum-like beat sounded from below. Bryce's shuffling feet marched along to the rhythm of the sound as he walked through the rocky tunnel. He and the doctor were being pulled farther below the surface by some powerful unseen force.

Bryce could see the shadowy outlines of others marching with them. Seven or eight others, all moving forward in complete silence. Some of the figures looked familiar to Bryce, but he couldn't remember their faces or their names.

He only remembered the doctor. He could see him clearly now, despite the darkness.

And he could see the golden chains around all of their wrists. Bryce was a prisoner. So was the doctor. But why?

Bryce felt like he was no longer in control of his actions. Some power had moved him like a puppet without strings. The power had forced him to enter the doctor's house and confront the doctor. To kidnap him.

But did I actually kidnap him? Bryce thought. After all, his own hands were chained, too. *What is going on?*

The drum pounded, and his feet obeyed. They all marched mindlessly along their hot, horrible journey. But who — or what — was beating that drum?

And where was Thora?

3

DARK TOWER

In Dr. Hoo's library, something strange was happening. The entire library shook. The four large windows of the octagonal room went black. A low hum vibrated through the air.

Thora fell to the floor in the middle of the doctor's library. *Why do I feel so dizzy?* she thought. *Is this some evil trick of the gathool?*

Louise collapsed into Thora's lap. The little girl stared up at her, her eyes wide and fearful.

"What's happening?" she pleaded, but Thora could barely hear her.

Thora glanced around for Pablo. She saw him on the nearby couch. He was trying to stand up, but he kept falling back onto the cushions.

Zak was still on his feet, but he jerked and wobbled like a puppet. He bent his knees and held his arms out for balance. Slowly, as if he were moving underwater, he trudged toward the library door.

"No!" screamed Mara. "Don't —"

Zak opened the door. A burst of red light and sound threw him backward into the room. A grinding roar shuddered through the building. Wind rushed through the door, blowing books off shelves, and stirring up cyclones of dust.

Thora shielded her face. She saw flashes of crimson light rushing past the library entrance as if they were on a merry-go-round.

"We're turning," Thora cried. "The building is turning!"

Mara staggered over to the door and slammed it shut. The wind stopped and the grinding sound quieted. She hurried over to Zak and kneeled, putting a hand on his shoulder. "Are you all right?" she asked.

"What is going on?" he demanded. "What was out there!?"

"The word on the wall — *croatoan*," Mara began. "The *gathool* warriors use the word whenever they need to leave a message behind for their comrades. It lets others know how to return home."

Pablo stood up from the couch. "Then we need to get there," he said.

Mara nodded. "But there is only one way to travel. By using ancient *gathool* technology. By using a *croatoan*."

Technology? Thora wondered. Then she remembered. In their most recent battle against the trolls, the creatures had been approaching the surface inside a weird tower-like vessel. It had risen through countless layers of rock and lava like a rocket made of stone.

"The tower is moving!" Thora exclaimed.

"Yes," said Mara. "I don't know how or why, but it must have something to do with the power inside each of you. The doctor always said you four are linked together."

"What do you mean?" Thora asked.

"Dr. Hoo said that his tower would react to your desires when the time came," Mara explained. "I didn't realize before now that Dr. Hoo's tower is a vessel that will take us into the heart of the *gathool* world."

Zak propped himself up on the floor. "So," he said, "this house is taking us to the trolls' realm?"

Mara smiled at him. "Yes," she said. "Your unified desire to save the doctor, and your friends and family, must have activated the tower gateway, or *croatoan*. Otherwise, it never would have moved."

Zak shook his head. "That's crazy," he said. "How can thoughts move an object? It's just not realistic."

"But Zak," said Thora, "think about what we've seen lately. The silo, the trolls, how we all . . . changed. Into warriors."

Zak hesitated. "I guess," he said. "I just figured we'd climb down some well, scare a few of the trolls, and then drag the doctor's butt back up here. Or . . . up there." He glanced up at the library's ceiling. "Uh, where exactly are we?"

Mara walked to a book sitting on a wooden stand in the center of the room. "I'm not sure," she replied. She flipped to the back of the book, reading the doctor's notes aloud. "'Reaching the entrance to the trolls' realm likely involves traveling through solid rock, of course, but also some kind of barrier. Something like a different dimension.'"

Zak rolled his eyes. "Every time you answer a question," he said, "you make even less sense."

"Maybe it's like a wormhole," suggested Pablo.

Everyone stared blankly at Pablo.

"You know," Pablo continued, "like, a single point that allows you to travel immediately across vast distances."

Thora arched an eyebrow and grinned. "Where did you hear about that?" she said.

Pablo smirked. "My dad and I used to watch a lot of *Star Trek* reruns," he said. "In one episode, Captain Picard said that wormholes were like secret passages between different parts of the universe." Pablo trailed off, suddenly embarrassed.

Thora smiled at Pablo. "I used to watch *Star Trek* too," she said warmly. Pablo smiled.

"Actually," Mara said, sounding impressed, "that's not very different from how the doctor explained it to me."

Louise was still lying next to Thora with her head in Thora's lap. "So . . . are we flying up?" Louise asked. "Or going down?"

Thora could tell Louise was scared and trying to hide it. "I don't know, Louise," Thora said. "But at least we're all together. Remember how you helped me back at the silo?"

"Sort of," said Louise. "I helped you lift that jar."

"Exactly," Thora said. "Your power of balance helped us win that fight."

Louise sat up, smiling. "Really? I helped us win?!" she asked. "Cool!"

Zak stood up, then he took a few steps and turned to Thora. "So where's that golden jar now?" he asked her.

Thora rolled her eyes. "It's not like I can pull it out of my pocket," she said.

"So where is it?" Zak repeated.

Pablo walked up to Zak. "Where's that bear I saw?" he challenged. "You know, Ursa Major."

"Oh yeah, the bear!" said Louise. She let out a little roar and started giggling.

Zak looked down at his chest and his arms. "Let's find out," he said. He closed his eyes tightly and took a few deep breaths. His face started to turn red as he tensed all his muscles.

Thora grinned. "What exactly are you trying to do?" she asked.

Zak opened his eyes and let out a breath. "I'm focusing, okay?" he said. "I thought maybe if I concentrated —"

"What?" interrupted Pablo. "You'd turn into a bear?"

Thora laughed.

Zak smirked. "Got any better ideas, Mr. Know-It-All?" he asked.

Pablo put his hand on Zak's shoulder. "Sorry," Pablo said. "But I just don't think it works that way."

"I think our powers work whenever we really need them," Thora suggested. "But that's just a guess."

Zak walked over to the couch and plopped down. "Great," he said. "What good are superpowers if you can't use them when you want to?"

Thora squinted hard at Zak's hands. She saw that his fingers were glowing.

A silver radiance was creeping up Zak's wrists and arms.

"Zak!" cried Thora.

Zak looked at her. "What, weirdo?"

"Zak!" said Louise.

"What is your problem?" Zak asked.

"Look at your hands!" Thora said.

Thora watched Zak look at his hands. His eyes went wide, and a smile slowly crept up the corners of his mouth. "It's happening!" he said.

"Thora!" cried Louise. "Look at me!" She stood. She seemed as tall as Mara now. Her hair was longer, and it flickered back and forth as if an invisible wind ran through it.

"Why is this happening now?" asked Thora.

Mara raised her hand, motioning for everyone to be quiet. They all listened. The faint grinding sound was gone. The library room had stopped moving. The windows, which had been dark rectangles before, now let in a faint reddish light from beyond. The light danced around them like flames.

One of the windows suddenly lit up with a bright red blaze. The glass shattered and went flying across the room.

Something in the window hissed at them. Louise screamed.

"*Agna gathool*," cried Mara. "Fire trolls!"

4
GATE OF FIRE

The troll known as Uzhk stopped at
the mouth of a new tunnel that sloped
downward at a steep angle. Uzhk peered
in and stared at the far end. He made a
strange sound in his throat that a human
may have thought sounded like a gulp.

This was the passageway that Uzhk
had been seeking ever since he left the
human farm far above him. The sight of
the great tower rising up from within the
abandoned silo had spurred him to come
this way.

Uzhk had seen similar vessels invading the surface before. Centuries ago, they had pierced through openings around the early American colonies. They had attacked armies on horseback in the far fields of Mongolia. The great vessels had soared upward into the Bermuda islands. Each time, they were defeated by *prak tara* — the children of the stars.

But Uzhk had learned a lesson from those battles. The *gathool,* his evil brethren, never attacked in just one place. More *gathool* warships, like the one beneath the silo, would be launched, and they would be carrying larger and deadlier warriors. He hoped he could reach the heart of the attacks, the ones who were sending the palaces of night into the world of humans. If he could somehow stop them from attacking the surface . . .

Uzhk stared hard at the far end of the tunnel. Golden light gleamed steadily at the exit. It was the barrier to the *gathool* kingdom, a wall of golden light. It was merely a tiny section of a powerful, glowing sphere that lay buried in the Earth's mantle. The sphere's wall was thin, Uzhk knew, thinner than a finger on his friend Mara's hand. "Thin as a piece of paper," Dr. Hoo had told him. But the golden light was deadly to all trolls, the evil *gathool* and Uzhk's *drakhool* brethren alike.

It had been many years since Uzhk had come this way, when he first left the kingdom of darkness for the world of light. The world of humans. Back then, he had help.

This time, he would have to pass through the wall by himself.

On the other side of the deadly wall were the two beings he had to find. One was a human. The other was the wearer of the Lava Crown, the general of the *gathool* army, the creature who had ordered the *gathool* invasion.

Uzhk struck his chest with his sledgehammer hands and bellowed out a war cry. He lowered his head and ran down the tunnel.

The steep angle added to his momentum. Faster and faster he ran. He cried out again. The golden rays seemed to burn into his rocky flesh. His eyes blazed with pain. He feared they would sizzle in their sockets and pop out of his skull. But he kept running. Then, in an instant, the giant figure passed into the gleaming golden curtain of light.

5

FIRE FIGHT

Two unearthly beings skittered through the broken library window. Their burning breaths moved the curtains by the window, causing the fabric to catch fire as the creatures passed by.

Pablo thought the creatures looked like upright lizards. They had sharp claws, several eyes, and thick scales. Their skin glowed orange-red like coals beneath a smoldering campfire.

How many different kinds of trolls are there?! he asked himself.

These ones looked like ferocious dinosaur-spiders.

Pablo, a voice whispered in Pablo's mind. The voice was warm and cozy, like a fireplace on a winter morning. *Pablo . . . you know nothing . . . you cannot stop us.*

"What?" Pablo yelled out loud.

The monstrous trolls emitted a terrifying collective hiss that each of the humans heard as a different sound. To Louise, the hiss sounded like her pet rabbit screaming. Zak heard the screech of tires as his parents cried out in pain. Thora heard her brother calling out for her help. Mara heard the doctor's voice calling her foolish for letting the children enter the realm of the trolls.

The hiss tore through Pablo's mind like a hot knife.

To him, the voice sounded like Thora, but it was far crueler than she'd ever been. "You stupid nerd," the voice howled. "It's your fault we're going to die here!"

The hiss stopped as a thunderous roar broke out beside him. The nimble trolls lurched back in surprise when a colossal silver bear reared up and roared, baring its gleaming fangs. Then the bear charged forward and swiped its massive paws at the trolls.

Pablo tried to warn Zak that the trolls might burn him, but the shout got caught in his throat. Somehow, his hand was once again grasping a sword, just as it had back at the silo.

Pablo smiled and dashed forward to fight alongside his friend, the marauding bear.

The huge bear and his warrior companion stood before the fire trolls, attacking them with claws and blades.

Suddenly, a troll hissed. Below its burning eyes, a mouth filled with jagged teeth opened wide. A jet of flame spurted from the troll's throat. "Look out!" shouted Pablo as he shoved the big bear to the side.

The fireball shot between him and Zak and burst into a bookshelf, turning it into a pile of smoldering ashes. Another stream of fire swooshed from the troll's jaws and missed Louise's long hair by mere inches. She ducked and jumped to the side, flying past Thora. She was hovering several feet above the floor!

Thora didn't have time to marvel at this new demonstration of the younger girl's powers.

Instead, Thora turned her attention to the fire trolls. They moved carefully and quickly, barely making a sound — except when they belched searing flames. Bookshelves, furniture, and scientific artifacts were all wreathed in fire. The library's ceiling had filled with smoke.

Mara had emerged from behind the bookcase. She was spraying a fire extinguisher on the table of Dr. Hoo's books. Thora ran to her and helped pat out flames that danced along the books' covers and spines.

Zak roared again and swung his paw at the fire trolls. Finally, he connected with one of the beasts and knocked the troll on its side. Searing pain ran up Zak's bear-arm all the way to his shoulder. His skin and fur burned.

Zak howled so loudly that the air quivered like heat rippling off a hot road. The reverberation caused the fallen troll's scales to crack and break. Hot magma oozed out of the dead troll's husk.

Pablo swung his sword at the second troll. He managed to slice off one of its limbs. When the troll opened its mouth and hissed, Pablo knew what was coming. He instinctively raised his left arm to protect himself — and a silver shield appeared. Its gleaming surface deflected the troll's flames and sent the fire back in the beast's face. However, the troll kept moving forward. Another troll crawled through the window and joined the fight.

Zak and I are barely slowing them down, thought Pablo. *The trolls might not kill us, but the fire will.*

Pablo turned to look for Thora. He saw her standing near the book table. Their eyes met. Pablo saw a sparkle in Thora's eyes. As if she could hear his thoughts, Thora gave Pablo a quick nod.

Suddenly, a rushing breeze passed through the room as pages from the books were lifted up in a whirlwind. The pages circled Thora like a cyclone of paper. She grew taller as the flying pages clung to her skin and transformed into a silver gown made of flowing fabric. Ornate armor seemed to grow around her torso. A gleaming helmet graced the top of her head. The jar from the previous battle was not in sight, but Pablo knew that didn't matter. Thora was ready for battle.

Thora lifted her chin and aimed her arms at one of the fire trolls.

A burst of wind sent the creature flying out the window and into the darkness.

Just then, Zak cried out in pain. Another slug had wrapped its long long tongue around Zak's bear-feet, tripping him to the ground. His furry skin sizzled where the tongue was latched onto his legs.

Pablo moved toward his friend and repeatedly hacked at the tongue with his sword. Another troll maneuvered itself behind Pablo. With his back to his enemy, he and Zak were left unprotected.

The troll's jaws opened. It began coughing up a glob of searing flame.

Then the entire room tilted toward the broken window. The trolls slid backward as the jet of flame erupted from the troll's roaring mouth.

Since the troll had been knocked off-balance, the fire flew wide of its aim, narrowly missing Zak and Pablo.

How? thought Pablo. He looked back to see Louise floating above the floor, smiling. She looked like a beautiful teenage girl wearing clothes from an ancient era. Her eyes were closed, but she was moving her hands up and down. It seemed as if she were causing the floor to shift like the deck of a ship in water.

A wide wave of silver water slammed against the trolls in the form of a huge tidal wave. Thora aimed her arms at the trolls and a gust of wind struck the water, directing waves past Zak and Pablo and toward the hideous slugs. Higher and higher the water rose within the library. Waves circled the room like a whirlpool.

The trolls were hurled through the glass and out the window in a gust of bright foam.

Then the water began to recede. It leaked out the walls, the door frame, and through cracks in the floorboards. Louise slowly settled back onto the floor, standing on her own feet again. She breathed a sigh of relief.

Pablo stood swordless, shaking his head, his Roman-style armor and weapons gone. Then he saw Zak. He was holding his legs in pain, buckled over on the floor.

"Are you okay?" Pablo asked, rushing toward his friend.

Zak shook his head. "I don't know," he said through clenched teeth. His skin was red and blistered where the troll's tongue had grabbed him.

Blood seeped from the gashes.

Thora and Mara ran over to him. "Maybe there's a first aid kit somewhere in the library," said Mara.

"No," said Thora calmly. "Let me." She reached out and gently touched Zak's ankles. He started to pull away in pain. "Hold still," Thora said, smiling. Her hand closed over his burns as she looked into Zak's eyes.

Thora's hand began to glow with a golden radiance.

"Ahh," Zak cried out.

"Help me," Thora said, looking first at Pablo, then at Louise. The two moved closer to Thora and placed their own hands on top of hers. The golden light from her hand grew instantly.

It wrapped around Zak's ankles and began to enclose all of their hands. Soon, all four friends were encased in a sphere of light. The golden glow turned to a bright silver.

Starlight, thought Pablo. Suddenly, a blinding flash burst through the room.

"My leg!" cried Zak. He blinked tightly. As he opened his eyes, he held his leg up for the others to see. His flesh was no longer red or burned. It was healed.

"Wow!" Zak said. Then he stared at Thora. "How'd you know how to do that?"

Thora shrugged and smiled. "Dunno, she said. "Instinct, I guess."

Zak shook his head in disbelief. "I never felt anything like that before."

Pablo nodded. He noticed his hand felt

empty and naked without a sword in it.

Pablo flexed his fingers. The thirst for battle was growing inside of him, even though the trolls were gone.

Pablo looked over at Mara. "Did you hear their voices?" he asked. "When they first attacked? Like, in your head?"

"We are in the *gathool*'s world now," Mara said. "Their powers are stronger here."

"Do you think they'll attack again?" Pablo asked.

"I don't know," said Mara. "But we have to move. The trolls know we're here now."

Zak smirked. "You think?" he said. "The giant fire-slug-lobster attack made that pretty obvious."

Louise stood. "The fire's out," she said

quietly. They all glanced around at the charred remains of the library.

Only one book had survived the flames. Mara cradled the *Book of Stars* in her arms.

Thora gazed out the windows. "There are fires burning everywhere in this world," she said.

Pablo wasn't surprised. He was sure they'd see much more fire — and fighting — before the day was over. They were in the trolls' world now.

"Well, we might as well do what we came here for," Zak said. "Let's go save the doctor."

6

Ooloom

Dr. Hoo shuffled along with the other humans.

Hroom . . . hroom . . .

His movements weren't controlled by the powerful drumbeat like the others were. He knew exactly where the pull of the *gathool* was taking them. He had been there many times before. But it was important that the other humans thought he was the *gathool*'s prisoner, just like they were.

Suddenly, the marching stopped. Bryce Gamble, Thora's brother, was next to him.

Farther back was Louise's father, Mr. Tooker, followed by Zak's parents, the Fishers.

They had all reached the entrance to the heart of the *gathool* kingdom. Their escort of powerful troll warriors stepped aside and pulled open the massive stone doors. The humans gasped and blinked at the countless crimson fires illuminating the jagged tunnel.

The entrance opened into a vast cavern a thousand times greater than any coliseum or stadium. Dr. Hoo saw Bryce gaze at it in awe. *This is his first time here,* Dr. Hoo thought. *He probably feels like an insect that's been plopped into the center of the old quarry outside Zion Falls. I know I did the first time I saw it.*

As the travelers moved forward, the tunnel emerged into a rocky bridge. The bridge led toward a gigantic mesa thrusting upward in the center. They had entered a volcano's magma chamber. The doctor glanced down the side of the bridge. Churning molten lava surrounded the mesa. Waves of lava rose and fell, crashing into each other in immense torrents of thundering flame. It was the source of the fiery light that illuminated the vast chamber.

The distant, curving walls were as tall as mountains. Lights and shadows played across their rocky surfaces, but the ceiling of the coliseum was draped in shadows and darkness.

HROOM . . . HROOM . . .

The pulsing beat grew louder.

The humans marched involuntarily across the narrow causeway, heading for the mesa's heart. Fear was written all over their faces, but they could not resist the beat of the drum.

Something glowed at the center of the raised rock, but it was still too far for anyone to see. The doctor knew they were close to its source, which gave it even more power.

Ooloom, a voice whispered inside the doctor's head. *Bow to Ooloom.*

The humans looked at each other with confused glances. They all seemed to be asking themselves, "Did the others hear it?"

Then the whisper came again. *All hail Ooloom,* it said. *The wearer of the Lava Crown.*

Onward they marched, wide-eyed and fearful. Walls of heat rose upward from the vast sea and shimmered past them. Several times the doctor thought Bryce might faint, but the relentless drum pulled him forward anyway.

Hroom . . . Ooloom . . .

Unlike Dr. Hoo, the other humans didn't know that the drumming sound was in their heads. It was a psychic whisper that the wearer of the Lava Crown sent into their minds, compelling them to come to him. The closer they were, the stronger his influence on them would be. A cold chill slid across the back of Dr. Hoo's neck. He felt the Lava Crown's influence beginning to affect him as well.

As they neared the center of the mesa, they all saw the glowing object at the center.

A brilliant statue, with veins pulsing like lava, sat atop the great mesa. The humans all gasped and trembled. Atop its head rested a glowing ring of magma fashioned in the shape of a crown. Even the sight made Dr. Hoo shrink back. Its power was immense. Vast.

Dr. Hoo saw Bryce close his eyes as the fear burned within him. All the humans were starting to feel an overpowering sense of fear and dread. *It's fortunate the effect is half as strong for me,* Dr. Hoo thought. *Otherwise, I'd be powerless right now — just like them.*

A commotion behind Dr. Hoo distracted him from his thoughts. A troll was racing toward the center of the mesa.

Other trolls tried to stop the figure, but it was relentless.

It stormed forward, crushing and throwing aside everything in its path. The frantic creature looked as if it were carved from rock, with huge slabs for arms, and boulders in the place of shoulders and knees.

The troll kept pushing forward until it reached the front of the line — and the doctor. Dr. Hoo looked up into the creature's face and frowned. "Uzhk!" he said. "What are you doing here?!"

The troll uttered rough, rasping sounds. "We are brothers," Uzhk said in his own language. He lifted the Dr. Hoo's shirt, and pointed at the third arm protruding from his chest. The crowd of humans gasped at the strange sight. "We are brothers by blood and magma. Sons of one mother. Our voices speak the same tongue. Together, we can stop this war! Unite with me!"

The doctor stared sadly at the monster. He shook his head back and forth slowly. "I cannot," he said.

"But the *prak tara* —" said Uzhk.

The doctor raised his arms — all three of them — above his head and tensed his muscles. A flash of intense red light burst from his hands. Uzhk was hurled backward across the mesa. He crashed headlong onto the ground near the edge of a cliff, his face facing downward at the ocean of lava beneath them.

"We are . . . brothers," moaned the troll. Several cracks ran through his rocky figure. Molten lava seeped out from the wounds.

"We *were* brothers," the doctor said coldly. He gestured at his third arm. "But, as the saying goes, you've forced my hand."

Uzhk's rocky face turned dark. "Brother," he croaked. "Please don't turn your back on the *drakhool*. On the humans. On me."

Dr. Hoo turned to the other humans, ignoring Uzhk completely. He snapped his fingers. Instantly, the golden chains that were latched around his wrists vanished.

"Forward!" Dr. Hoo ordered the chained humans. "March . . . or die."

The doctor watched Bryce struggle against his bonds. The boy whimpered in pain as the gold seared his flesh whenever he moved.

"Forward!" Doctor Hoo repeated.

Suddenly, with a rumble that threw the humans off their feet, the glowing statue rose from its seated position. It stood tall before them, pulsing with dark energy.

It grew higher and higher, like a hill of stone. And the bright crown on top grew larger with it.

The creature's red eyes were made of molten lava. Lava also shone brightly in its mouth. Its massive chest heaved in and out. With each long, mighty throb, the drumbeat sounded in the humans' ears. Eerie words joined the rhythm. *Ooloom. Ooloom. Ooloom.*

Dr. Hoo knelt and bowed his head. Bryce glanced at the doctor's third arm.

"Who — *what* — are you?" Bryce sputtered. For a moment, Dr. Hoo looked hurt. But before he or Bryce could say anything more, the crowned giant slowly turned its gaze toward Bryce. The roar of scraping rocks filled the chamber. Then an ugly voice whispered into their minds.

He is. My servant, it said. *His task. Was to bring. You all. To me.*

A spark of fire shot upward from the Lava Crown. Bryce and the other humans cried out in pain and fell, unconscious, to the rocky floor.

The living rock wearing the crown spoke directly into Dr. Hoo's mind. *You have. Done well,* it said. *Deceiver.*

Dr. Hoo said nothing.

7
PRISONERS

The tunnel angled sharply downward. Thora and the others carefully traveled over stony ledges and rough ridges. The rocky floor of the tunnel felt hot beneath Thora's feet. The walls were warm against her palms when she leaned on them for support.

"I'm surprised we haven't seen more trolls so far," Thora said.

Zak grunted. "I'm not," he said. "They are probably just waiting for us to come to them."

In the tunnel's dim light, Mara held the *Book of Stars* close to her face, trying to make out the ancient scrawls traced on the book's final pages. "If I'm reading this map correctly," she said in a hushed voice, "then we're almost there."

Thora knew they were approaching their goal without having to read a map. She could sense the looming threat, and they were starting to respond physically.

Louise's voice had changed, seeming more mature. The younger girl holding Thora's hand was growing taller, too.

Pablo's silhouette, up ahead, now included a helmet and swords.

Thora felt a new weight grow upon her shoulders as her armor started to appear once again.

"How's your arm doing, Zak?" she asked. The boy behind her merely growled. She turned, and saw that Zak had the head and arms of a bear.

"That's a good look for you," Thora teased. A gruff noise that sounded vaguely like a laugh came from Zak's throat.

Suddenly, Thora heard a familiar voice echo in her mind.

Thora . . . help me . . .

Thora had heard Bryce's voice in her head once before — just outside the doctor's house. Bryce had whispered to her, asking her for help. She didn't know it was him at the time. Back then, Bryce's voice had sounded strained and twisted — not like him at all. This time was different. He sounded like himself now.

Thora knew he was in danger. She knew he needed her help.

"Bryce is here!" she said. She raced down the sloping tunnel toward the exit. The others quickly followed.

Soon, they plunged out of the darkness and into a vast, fiery chamber. Waves of burning magma thundered and rolled on every side. Thora didn't stop. She kept running along the bridge.

Please . . . help me . . . Thora . . .

"Bryce!" Thora yelled. "Where are you?!"

"Thora, stop!" cried Mara.

Hideous creatures stood on both sides of Thora's path, but they didn't move to stop her. Their eyes were turned toward the center of the massive mesa. That's where she was heading.

That's where Bryce is, Thora thought. *I will save you this time, big bro.*

The others ran hard, trying to catch up with her.

As Thora neared the center of the mesa, she saw a gigantic statue with a flaming crown atop its head. At the statue's feet was a group of humans lying on their sides. All of them had golden chains around their hands and legs. Nearest to her lay Bryce, his eyes barely open.

"Bryce!" screamed Thora. She ran up and kneeled next to her brother.

"Bryce," she whispered. "Are you all right?"

Bryce's pale face gazed up at her. "Thora?" he asked uncertainly.

Thora felt the helmet on her head.

Her transformation was complete. *I guess I look pretty different right now,* she thought. "Yes, it's me," she said.

Bryce lifted a hand toward her strange armor. With his finger, he traced an engraving of swirling stars that decorated her chestplate. He smiled weakly. "Wow," he said.

Thora smiled. "Everything's going to be all right, big bro," she said.

Bryce began to shiver. "I . . . I did this," he said. "I brought us all here. Into this trap. I'm . . . I'm so sorry."

Ooloom. A voice pounded in Thora's ears. Thora looked up and gasped as the statue shifted toward her. She felt its burning eyes, bright as comets, reach deep inside her core.

Just then, the others caught up to Thora. They stood behind her, uncertain of what to do.

Then, out from behind the monstrous troll's leg, stepped a familiar figure. "Doctor!" shouted Mara.

Dr. Hoo now stood several paces away from where Bryce lay. He walked toward the young warriors, confusion and surprise covering their faces.

"Doc!" Zak said. "We're here to rescue you!" Zak was now a bear, and his voice came out gruff and deep.

The doctor recognized him. He smiled wide. Then he raised his three arms upward. Instantly, the mesa exploded in scarlet brilliance.

Everyone fell to the ground.

Thora cried out in pain. She looked up at the doctor in horror. "What are you . . . doing?" she whimpered.

Ooloom. The giant troll gazed down at the fallen humans. A thunderous voice bellowed throughout the entire chamber. "You have. Done well," the giant troll said. It looked at Dr. Hoo, adding, "My servant."

The doctor bowed his head. All three of his hands were open and held out toward the giant creature.

The young warriors' eyes all went wide. "No!" Zak growled. "It's not possible! You can't be one of them!"

A hiss reverberated throughout the vast chamber, growing louder and louder. It seemed to circle them like an evil wind. Thora heard more voices join in the sinister sound. The hissing grew louder.

"Uzhk!" Mara cried. She pointed toward the edge of the mesa where it dropped off into the lava sea. A strange-looking troll lay there, collapsed.

Then Thora saw more figures just beyond the collapsed troll. The entire mesa was ringed in a curtain of dark shadows. It was a multitude of trolls.

Monstrous, many-headed, many-handed beings all marched toward the Lava Crown. The circle of warriors grew tighter as they surrounded the powerless humans. This hiss they cried out was deafening.

The giant nodded his colossal head, his crown sputtering with flames. He spoke to his subjects. "*Prak tara marith yoo,*" the giant rumbled. The giant troll looked at the young heroes, then at the doctor. "The children of the stars must die."

The doctor nodded. He raised his arms once again. A golden light appeared above their heads, spinning like a disc. The light separated into distinct rings, forming a long, golden chain.

Slowly, the chain floated down toward the young heroes and landed on the ground with a thud. Before they could react, the shackles connected around their hands and their feet, chaining them.

The army of a million trolls marched forward. The ring grew tighter. Thora saw the *Book of Stars* lying face down on the ground where Mara had dropped it.

Thora remembered the words the doctor had read to them from it, that first night in his house. The ancient prophecies talked about a band of gold that would defeat the trolls. These shackles were bands of gold.

The doctor lied to us, Thora thought. *He tricked us.*

Suddenly Zak growled. "Mom, Dad!" he yelled. He lurched forward, but the chain sizzled around his limbs and brought him crashing painfully to the ground. He howled in pain.

Thora saw the Fishers among the crowd of human prisoners lying on the ground. They were unconscious, but breathing.

Bands of gold, Thora thought, noticing their chains. *The doctor captured us all with bands of gold.*

Zak lay on his side, racked with pain. He strained to reach his arm out toward his parents. "I have to . . . help them," he whimpered. The chains sizzled around his limbs.

Hate burned inside Thora. She glared at the doctor, watching him bow his head as he kneeled toward the crowned troll.

"You traitor!" Thora yelled.

8

HEART OF STONE

Dr. Hoo rose into the air over the heads of the young humans, red waves of light emanating from him. Bryce watched the bottoms of the doctor's shoes recede as he rose higher and higher into the air. Soon, the doctor was face to face with the fiery giant.

As the giant's gaze turned toward Dr. Hoo and away from the humans, Bryce felt momentary relief. He could breathe again without pain.

But the troll army's feet still shook the ground as the trolls continued to close the circle around the humans.

Another hot gust of wind blew across the mesa as the giant spoke to the hovering doctor. "You have. Brought them," he growled. "For me."

"Yes, Ooloom," Dr. Hoo said. "As a gift for you."

Ooloom, Bryce thought. The name made him shiver despite the heat.

"A sacrifice," Ooloom bellowed. "To me."

"Just as you deserve," Dr. Hoo said. "Ooloom, Wearer of the Lava Crown."

Bryce looked at his sister. He could tell Thora's pain had also lessened, but her face was still twisted in agony.

Thora was staring at the golden shackles around their limbs with disgust. She caught Bryce's gaze and whispered, "He betrayed us all. He made a deal with that . . . monster."

Bryce clenched his teeth. *He did this,* he thought. *The doctor betrayed my sister.* Furious, he strained against his chains, trying to break them. Instead, it just pulled the chains taut against all four heroes. They let out a collective scream as the golden shackles seared into their skin.

Ooloom laughed, lava spitting out from his rocky lips. "There is. No escape," he growled.

Bryce glanced at Dr. Hoo. There was a pained look on the doctor's face. *Wait,* the doctor whispered into Bryce's mind. *Wait.*

Bryce's eyes went wide.

What does he mean? Bryce thought. He turned to see Thora looking at him with wide eyes. *She heard it too.*

Ooloom turned his gaze back to the doctor. His voice rumbled throughout the fiery cavern. "You too. Must bow. To Ooloom."

The doctor smiled widely and spread his three arms out in a gesture of peace and submission. "I have always obeyed those who are more powerful than me," Dr. Hoo said.

Ooloom's laugh sounded like gravel and roaring fire. "You are. Very weak," he said.

"I have never been as strong as you, Ooloom," Dr. Hoo said. "I am only half-troll, unlike you. But I take comfort in the power of my ancestors."

"Words. Words," replied the giant. "You bore. Ooloom."

"Words can be power," Dr. Hoo said calmly. "The *gathool* have always respected power, am I correct?"

Ooloom stiffened. "Yes," he said reluctantly. "It is. Our way."

The doctor closed his eyes and bowed his head. He began chanting a rhyme:

"Fiercer than lava,

Stronger than stone,

Harder than iron,

Brighter than bone.

Sharper than teeth

Deeper than fear —

Answer this, friend,

And see it appear."

Dr. Hoo nodded almost imperceptibly at Bryce. Then he turned to face Ooloom. "The ancient riddle," Dr. Hoo said, "reminds us of the greatest power. What is fiercer than lava? What is deeper than fear?"

The giant began to sway back and forth. The Lava Crown glowed an angry red. "Silence!" he growled.

"Friend," Thora whispered to Bryce. "The answer is friend."

Answer this, friend, and see it appear, Bryce repeated in his mind. *Friend. By speaking the word 'friend', you identify yourself as one. Thora was right.*

Bryce nodded. "He's distracted," he said. "Now's our chance."

Thora nodded. She grabbed Bryce's hand and held it tightly.

The chains burned her, but she silently strained against them and reached for Pablo's foot. "Pablo," she whispered. "Grab on to Louise."

Pablo nodded. He quietly shifted his body and reached over to Louise.

"The band of gold," whispered Thora. "Companions. *Friends.* We have to close the circle."

Bryce felt another hand touch his shoulder. He looked over and saw Louise was leaning across the ground, reaching for him. The band of gold was almost complete.

The trolls moved closer. The rhythmic beating grew louder. A blaze of light erupted from the Lava Crown, high above the humans.

"No more talk," Ooloom warned the doctor.

The giant returned his gaze to the humans. His eyes flared. And like a pack of dying animals, the six companions howled in pain. "*Prak tara marith yoo,*" said the giant. "The stars. Will fall. And die."

Bryce had never felt such pain. But he held his grip as burning needles stabbed at his brain and his lungs. His skin felt as if it were being pulled from his bones.

Ooloom looked at his army of trolls. "Kill them. Now," he ordered.

The thudding of the troll army surrounded Thora, Pablo, Louise, Zak, and Bryce. The trolls lifted their axes, spears, and clubs over their heads, but the young warriors continued to concentrate.

The doctor's eyes went wide. Time was running out for the young warriors.

Then, suddenly, a rolling shadow ran through the line of troll warriors, sending several trolls flying off the edge of the mesa. It hurtled toward the bodies of the young humans like a storm cloud.

"Uzhk!" screamed Mara. The friendly troll ran and threw himself at Ooloom's left foot. He swung his fists into the giant's legs as hard as he could. *That troll's powerful,* thought Bryce. *But there's no way he could harm that monster.* But the diversion was enough. The giant's gaze was averted and the pain began to leak away. The young warriors focused again.

Suddenly, a wave of comfort beamed down upon them. It felt like warm sunlight on Bryce's pale skin.

He heard a sizzling sound. The golden chains were melting. They dripped harmlessly off their wrists and ankles into puddles of shining liquid at their feet.

"We're free," cried Bryce.

"Keep holding on to each other!" yelled Thora.

Ooloom growled. "Kill. The traitor!"

The troll warriors aimed at Uzhk from all sides. Instantly, shadows flew overhead as a shower of spears streamed toward Uzhk.

The friendly troll cried out as the weapons pierced his hide.

With a mighty shrug of his giant foot, Ooloom threw Uzhk aside. Then, with a colossal roar, Ooloom's foot rushed downward.

The gigantic, jagged foot crushed Uzhk beneath a ton of living rock. A rocky hand and fingers poked out from under the foot. They were motionless.

"Uzhk!" Dr. Hoo yelled. "No!"

9

THE BAND OF LIGHT

Louise began to steadily glow. A voice rang out among the humans. "Louise, is that you?" it said.

The girl saw her father, tears streaming down his cheeks. One of his arms hung limply at his side. Louise smiled at him. *Father!* she thought. She closed her eyes and focused as hard as she could.

The doctor dropped to the ground and grasped her hand. He smiled warmly at the others.

"Focus now," Dr. Hoo said. "We're running out of time."

Dr. Hoo bowed his head and closed his eyes. The others did the same. The band of friends was now complete. All of the companions began to glow with their former radiance.

The doctor raised his hands. The golden chains that held them together broke apart and floated above them. The chains spun swiftly, turning into a blur of light. Then they became one great circle of gold, forming a huge disc. The disc turned on end and started to spin. Slowly at first, and then faster and faster, until a faint whirring sound filled the chamber.

"The band of gold," said the doctor. "Companions of light."

All of them stared at the whirling disc. As it spun faster, it began absorbing the warriors' silver radiance. It began to gleam with a blinding combination of white light.

Like the sun, thought Louise. *A band of light!*

The white disc hummed. It moved above Ooloom's crown like a brilliant halo. Suddenly, a tremendous burst of energy erupted across the mesa.

Louise heard a horrible scream as the fiery crown exploded in a torrent of sparks and scarlet light. Cracks began to run along Ooloom's sides. Suddenly, magma spilled from the cracks and onto the ground as the monster split into several pieces, each of them tumbling lifelessly to the ground.

The disc, bright as a star, shifted its position to directly above the troll army. The horrid warriors began to stiffen. Then the army came to a sudden stop, petrified.

Zak jumped to his feet. "Yes!," he cried, human again. "We defeated their ruler!"

The doctor shook his head, grimly. "No," he said. "Not their ruler." He looked at the petrified giant. "He was merely their general. Their ruler, the Great One, lies far beyond this sea of lava."

The waves of lava surrounding the mesa rushed angrily against the cliffs. Dr. Hoo turned to face the young warriors. "Hurry," he said. "We must leave before the Great One comes."

Mara grabbed his shoulder. "Your tower is damaged," she said. "It will not be able to return us to the surface."

"No matter," said Dr. Hoo. He raised his hands. The golden disc slowly changed shape. Now it resembled a golden bowl. "Get everyone inside," he said.

All of the humans — including Zak's parents, Louise's father, and all the others — climbed into the golden vessel.

Once inside, Pablo grabbed Dr. Hoo by the arm. "We thought you betrayed us!" Pablo said. His arm was shaking. The others were listening intently.

Dr. Hoo put his hand on Pablo's shoulder. "I'm sorry, but I had to do it," he said. "Otherwise, the trolls would never have allowed you to get this close to Ooloom. The army would've destroyed you all."

"You still could've told us the plan," Thora said.

"Again, I'm sorry — but I really couldn't," the doctor explained. "The only way they would've allowed you inside this chamber is if you were their prisoners. It had to look real, or they would've killed you on sight."

Dr. Hoo stood. "I know I put you through a lot," he said. "But this was the only way to stop Ooloom. His army was preparing to march. They would've destroyed your homes." He glanced around, opening his arms at the family members and friends. "It was also the only way we could save your families. Your loved ones."

Everyone grew silent at the Doctor's words. The Gambles and the Fishers embraced their sons and daughters.

Mr. Tooker brushed Louise's hair from her face. "I can't believe it," he said, smiling down at her. "My little girl is a hero. I'm so proud of you." Louise dug her face into her father's chest, sobbing and smiling.

Dr. Hoo watched the scene. A faint smile crossed his face for a moment, then disappeared. He raised his arms into the air, and the golden bowl began to rise.

10

ASCENT

Everyone was silent as the golden bowl began its ascent. In the quiet, the bowl's humming could be heard. It rose high above the mesa floor, up and up into the vast darkness of the great chamber.

Mara took one last look, peering over the edge of the bowl. She gazed down at the dwindling island within the fiery sea, the resting place of her old friend. "Oh, Uzhk," she whispered.

Mara felt a hand on her shoulder.

Dr. Hoo was standing behind Mara, tears filling his eyes. He stared down at the boiling lava. Even from this great height they could feel the heat from the molten sea against their faces.

"Uzhk had a powerful heart," Dr. Hoo said. "An almost human one."

Mara stared into the doctor's eyes, seeking answers. "Was his death worth this victory?" she asked.

Dr. Hoo looked upward. "It has to be worth it," he said grimly. "Because this war is far from over."

Darkness closed in on them as the disc continued its ascent toward the surface.

About the Author

As a boy, MICHAEL DAHL persuaded his friends to celebrate the Norse gods associated with the days of the week. (Thursday was Thor's Day, his favorite!) Dahl has written the popular Library of Doom series, the Dragonblood books, and the Finnegan Zwake series. As a Norwegian lad from the Midwest, he believes in trolls.

ABOUT THE ILLUSTRATOR

BEN KOVAR was born in London. He trained in film and animation and spent several years as an animator and art director before moving into writing and illustrating fiction. He lives in an attic, likes moisture, and has a fear of sunlight and small children.

Notes on Gathool Leadership

"The strongest of trolls need not even open his mouth to challenge for leadership. Rather, the beating of his massive heart shakes the earth so fiercely that all other trolls are forced to their knees."

— from Hroom, Hroom by Anthony Atwood Crake

Above all else, trolls respect power. To become an Ooloom, or leader of the gathool army, a troll must prove he is stronger than all the rest. That is no easy task, considering that every troll is expected to do battle from the point they're able to lift a spear until the day they die.

The crowning of an Ooloom is a fearsome event. All challengers for leadership of the troll army present themselves as candidates. They choose their weapons, and the group melee begins. At the end of the chaotic battle, the last gathool standing has the Lava Crown placed atop his head, identifying him as the Ooloom. The title lasts until death - whether from old age, or at the hands of another troll looking to take his place.

Only Thooloom — or the Great One — has more power and influence over the gathool than an Ooloom. However, no one has seen the horrible Thooloom and lived to tell the tale...

The Gathool Vocabulary

The gathool language doesn't have many words, and the pronunciation is usually straightforward. However, many gathool words have several meanings, so translating the language is quite a challenge. Here are some of the words I've managed to decipher...

HOOLOO (hoo-LOO)—one with two souls. An individual who is born from one troll parent and one human parent. Also referred to as a half-blood.

HROOM (har-OOM)—there is no standard definition for this word. It sounds like a drum, and serves as a rally cry for powerful troll leaders.

OOLOOM (oo-LOOM)—harvester of souls. Ooloom is an honorary title given to the leader of the troll army. Only a Thooloom, also known as The Great One, commands more power and respect.

PRAK TARA (PROK TAR-uh)—the bearers of light. The phrase refers to the children of the stars, or the star-touched ones, who are fated to oppose the trolls in a grand battle for control of Earth.

Benjamin K. Hoo

FROM TROLL HUNTERS: BOOK 4

FALLEN STAR

Hundreds of townspeople from Zion Falls had fled from their burning homes. All of them now stood at the very edge of the quarry, side by side, in a long line. *Like an army,* thought Pablo.

"They're really close to the edge of the cliff," said Thora. "I hope nobody falls."

Just then, the entire line of townspeople bent down in unison. They reached their hands toward the ground, grabbing items Pablo couldn't quite see.

"Are they coming to help us?" asked Louise.

Pablo squinted into the distance. He saw what looked like pitchforks and flaming torches in the hands of the townspeople. "No," said Pablo, pulling Louise close to him. "They're coming to attack us."